ALESSANDRO BARICCO was born in Turin in
1958. He has written four novels (*Lands of Glass, Ocean
Sea, Silk* and *City*) all of which have been translated
into English, as well as two plays and two collections
of essays.

ANN GOLDSTEIN is a frequent and highly revered
translator from the Italian. Past translations include
Ocean Sea and *City* by Alessandro Baricco, *A Weakness
for Almost Everything* and *Journey to the Land of the Flies*
by Aldo Buzzi, *Pushkin's Button* by Serena Vitale, and
In the Name of Ishmael by Giuseppe Genna.

Without Blood

ALESSANDRO BARICCO

Translated from the Italian by Ann Goldstein

CANONGATE
Edinburgh · New York · Melbourne

First published in Great Britain in 2004 by
Canongate Books Ltd, 14 High Street,
Edinburgh, EH1 1TE

This edition published in 2005

10 9 8 7 6 5 4 3 2 1

Originally published in Italian as *Senza Sangue*
by Rizzoli, Milan

EDIMBURGO

This English translation was supported by
The Italian Cultural Institute, Edinburgh

British Library Cataloguing-in-Publication Data
A catalogue record for this book is available on
request from the British Library

ISBN 1 84195 574 4

Page design by Chong Weng-ho
Printed and bound by Clays Ltd, St Ives plc

The events and persons mentioned in this story are imaginary
and make no reference to any particular reality. The frequent
choice of Spanish names is due purely to their music and is not
intended to suggest a temporal or geographical location
of the action.

www.canongate.net

WITHOUT BLOOD

THE old farmhouse of Mato Rujo stood blankly in the countryside, carved in black against the evening light, the only stain in the empty outline of the plain.

The four men arrived in an old Mercedes. The road was pitted and dry—the mean street of the countryside. Manuel Roca saw them from the farmhouse.

He went to the window. First he saw the column of dust rising against the corn. Then he heard the sound of the engine. No one around here had a car anymore. Manuel Roca knew that. He saw the Mercedes emerge in the distance and disappear behind a line of oaks. Then he stopped looking.

He returned to the table and placed a hand on his daughter's head. 'Get up,' he told her. He took a key from his pocket, put it on the table, and nodded at his son. 'Yes,' the son said. They were children, just two children.

AT the crossroads where the stream ran the old Mercedes did not turn off to the farmhouse but continued towards Álvarez instead. The four men travelled in silence. The one driving had on a sort of uniform. The other man sitting in front wore a cream-coloured suit. Ironed. He was smoking a French cigarette. 'Slow down,' he said.

MANUEL Roca heard the sound fade into the distance towards Álvarez. Who do they think they're fooling? he thought. He saw his son come back into the room with a gun in his hand and another under his arm. 'Put them there,' he said. Then he turned to his daughter. 'Come, Nina. Don't be afraid. Come here.'

THE well-dressed man put out his cigarette on the dashboard of the Mercedes, then told the one who was driving to stop. 'This is good, here,' he said. 'And shut off this infernal engine.' He heard the slide of the hand brake, like a chain falling into a well. Then nothing. It was as if the countryside had been swallowed up in an unalterable silence.

'It would have been better to go straight there,' said one of the two sitting in back. 'Now he'll have time to run,' he said. He had a gun in his hand. He was only a boy. They called him Tito.

'He won't run,' said the well-dressed man. 'He's had it with running. Let's go.'

MANUEL Roca moved aside some baskets of fruit, bent over, raised a hidden trapdoor, and looked in. It was little more than a big hole dug into the earth, like the den of an animal.

'Listen to me, Nina. Now, some people are coming, and I don't want them to see you. You have to hide in here, the best thing is for you to hide in here and wait until they go away. Do you understand?'

'Yes.'

'You just have to stay here quietly.'

She stared.

'Whatever happens, you mustn't come out, you

mustn't move, just stay quietly here and wait.'

She said nothing.

'Everything will be all right.'

'Yes.'

'Listen to me. It's possible that I might have to go away with these men. Don't come out until your brother comes to get you, do you understand? Or until you can tell that no one is there and it's all over.'

'Yes.'

'I want you to wait until no one is there.'

The child stared.

'Don't be afraid, Nina, nothing's going to happen to you. All right?'

'Yes.'

'Give me a kiss.'

The girl pressed her lips against her father's forehead. He caressed her hair.

'Everything will be all right, Nina.'

He remained standing there, as if there were still something he had to say, or do.

'This isn't what I intended,' he said. 'Remember, always, that this is not what I intended.'

4

Instinctively, the child searched her father's eyes for something that might help her understand. She saw nothing. Her father leaned over and kissed her on the lips.

'Now go, Nina. Go on, down there.'

The child let herself fall into the hole. The earth was hard and dry. She lay down.

'Wait, take this.'

The father handed her a blanket. She spread it on the dirt, and lay down again.

She heard her father say something to her, then she saw the trapdoor lowered. She closed her eyes and opened them. Blades of light filtered through the floorboards. She heard the voice of her father as he went on speaking to her. She heard the sound of the baskets dragged across the floor. It grew darker under there. Her father asked her something. She answered. She was lying on one side. She had bent her legs, and she was there, curled up, as if she were in her bed, with nothing to do but go to sleep, and dream. She heard her father say something else, gently, leaning down to the floor. Then she heard a shot, and the sound of a window breaking into a thousand pieces.

'ROCA!...COME OUT, ROCA...DON'T DO ANYTHING STUPID AND COME OUT.'

Manuel Roca looked at his son. He crept over to the boy, careful not to move into the open. He reached for the gun on the table.

'Get away from there! Go and hide in the woodshed. Don't come out, don't make a sound, don't do anything. Take the gun and keep it loaded.'

The child stared at him without moving.

'Go on. Do what I tell you.'

But the child took a step towards him.

Nina heard a hail of shots sweep the house. Dust and bits of glass slid along the cracks in the floor. She didn't move. She heard a voice calling from outside.

'SO, ROCA. DO WE HAVE TO COME AND GET YOU? I'M SPEAKING TO YOU, ROCA. DO I HAVE TO COME AND GET YOU?'

The child was standing there, in the open. He had taken his gun, but was holding it in one hand, pointing it down and swinging it back and forth.

'Go,' said the father. 'Did you hear me? Get out of here.'

The child went towards him. What he was thinking was that he would kneel on the floor, and be embraced by his father. He imagined something like that.

The father pointed the gun at him. He spoke in a low, fierce voice.

'Go, or I'll kill you myself.'

Nina heard that voice again.

'LAST WARNING, ROCA.'

Gunfire fanned the house, back and forth like a pendulum, as if it would never end, back and forth like the beam of a lighthouse over a coal-black sea, patiently.

Nina closed her eyes. She flattened herself against the blanket, and curled up even tighter, pulling her knees to her chest. She liked to be in that position. She felt the earth, cool, under her side, protecting her—it would not betray her. And she felt her own curled-up body, folded around itself like a shell—she liked this—she was shell and animal, shelter of herself, she was everything, she was everything for herself, nothing could hurt her as long as she remained in this position. She reopened her eyes, and thought, Don't move, you're happy.

Manuel Roca saw his son disappear behind the door. Then he raised himself just enough to glance out the window. All right, he thought. He moved to another window, rose, aimed quickly, and fired.

The man in the cream-coloured suit cursed and threw himself to the ground. 'Look at this bastard,' he said. He shook his head. 'What about this son of a bitch?' He heard two more shots arrive from the farmhouse. Then he heard the voice of Manuel Roca.

'FUCK OFF, SALINAS.'

The man in the cream-coloured suit spat. 'Go fuck yourself, you bastard.' He glanced to his right and saw that El Gurre was sneering, flattened behind a stack of wood. He was holding a machine gun in his right hand, and with his left he searched his pocket for a cigarette. He didn't seem to be in a hurry. He was small and thin, he wore a dirty hat on his head and on his feet enormous mountain clogs. He looked at Salinas. He found the cigarette. He put it between his lips. Everyone called him El Gurre. He got up and began shooting.

Nina heard the burst of gunfire sweep the house, above her. Then silence. And immediately afterward another burst, longer. She kept her eyes open. She looked at the cracks in the floor. She looked at the light, and the dust that came from up there. Every so often she saw a shadow pass, and that was her father.

Salinas crawled over beside El Gurre, behind the woodpile.

'How long would it take Tito to get in?'

El Gurre shrugged his shoulders. He still had the sneer on his face. Salinas glanced at the farmhouse.

'We'll never get in from here: either he does it or we're in shit.'

El Gurre lit the cigarette. Then he said that the kid was quick and would manage it. He said that he knew how to creep like a snake and that they would have to trust him.

Then he said: 'Now we'll make a little distraction.'

Manuel Roca saw El Gurre emerge from behind the woodpile and throw himself to the ground. The machine-gun volley arrived punctually, prolonged. I've got to get out of here, he thought. Ammunition. First ammunition, then crawl to the kitchen and from there straight for the fields. Would they have someone behind the house? El Gurre isn't stupid, he must have someone there, too. But no one's firing from that direction. If someone were there, he would be firing. Maybe El Gurre isn't in charge. Maybe it's that coward Salinas. If it's Salinas, I can manage. He doesn't understand anything, Salinas. Stay behind your desk, Salinas, it's the only thing you know how to do. Go screw yourself. First the ammunition.

El Gurre was shooting.

Ammunition. And money. Maybe I can take the money with me, too. I should have run immediately, that's what I should have done. God damn. Now I've got to get out of here, if only he would stop for a second. Where did he get a machine gun, they have a car and a machine gun. Too much, Salinas.

The ammunition. Now the money.

El Gurre fired.

Nina heard the windows pulverise under the machine-gun shots. Then leaves of silence between one burst and the next. In the silence, the shadow of her father crept between the glass. With one hand she adjusted her skirt. She was like an artisan intent on refining his work. Curled on her side, she began eliminating the imprecisions one by one. She lined up her feet until she felt her legs perfectly coupled, the two thighs softly joined, the knees like two cups one inside the other, the calves barely separated. She checked the symmetry of her shoes, paired as if in a shop window, but on their sides, you might have said *lying down*, out of exhaustion. She liked that orderliness. If you are a shell, order is important. If you are shell and animal, everything has to be perfect. Precision will save you.

She heard the pounding of a long volley. And right afterward the voice of a boy.

'Put down that gun, Roca.'

Manuel Roca turned his head. He saw Tito standing a few yards away. He was pointing a pistol at him.

'Put down that gun and don't move.'

From outside came another burst of gunfire. But the boy didn't move, he stood there, gun pointed. Under that rain of shots, the two stood motionless, staring at each other, like a single animal that had stopped breathing. Manuel Roca, half lying on the floor, looked the boy in the eyes, as he stood there, in the open. He tried to comprehend if the boy was a child or a soldier, if it was his thousandth time or his first, and if there was a brain attached to that gun or only blind instinct. He saw the barrel of the gun tremble just perceptibly, as if it were making a tiny scribble in the air.

'Stay calm, kid,' he said.

Slowly he placed the rifle on the floor. With a kick he sent it sliding into the centre of the room.

'Everything's OK, kid,' he said.

Tito didn't take his eyes off him.

'Quiet, Roca, and don't move.'

Another blast arrived. El Gurre was working methodically. The boy waited until he finished, without lowering his gun or his gaze. When silence returned, he glanced towards the window.

'SALINAS! I'VE GOT HIM. STOP IT, I'VE GOT HIM.'

And after a moment:

'It's Tito. I've got him.'

'He's done it. Shit,' said Salinas.

El Gurre made a kind of smile, without turning. He was observing the barrel of the machine gun as if he had carved it himself, in idle hours, from the branch of an ash tree.

Tito looked for them in the light from the window.

Slowly Manuel Roca got up just enough so that he could lean his back against the wall. He thought of the gun pressing into his side, stuck in his pants. He tried to remember if it was loaded. He touched it with one hand. The boy didn't notice anything.

'Let's go,' Salinas said. They went around the stack of wood and headed straight for the farmhouse. Salinas walked slightly bent, as he had seen it done in films. He was ridiculous like all men who fight: without realising it. They were crossing the farmyard when they heard, from inside, a gunshot.

El Gurre ran. He reached the door of the farmhouse and kicked it open. Three years earlier, he had kicked open the door of the stable, had entered and had seen his wife hanging from the ceiling, and his two daughters with their heads shaved, their thighs spattered with blood.

He kicked open the door and went in and saw Tito, pointing the gun towards a corner of the room.

'I had to do it. He has a gun,' the boy said.

El Gurre looked in the corner. Roca was lying on his back. He was bleeding from one arm.

'I think he has a gun,' the boy said again. 'Hidden somewhere,' he added.

El Gurre went over to Manuel Roca.

He looked at the wound in his arm. Then he looked the man in the face.

'Hello, Roca,' he said.

He placed one shoe on Roca's wounded arm and began to crush it. Roca shrieked with pain and folded over on himself. The gun slid out of his pants. El Gurre leaned down to pick it up.

'You're a smart kid,' he said. Tito nodded. He realised that he still had his arm extended in front of him, and the gun in his hand, pointed at Roca. He lowered it. He felt his two fingers relax around the trigger of the pistol. His whole hand hurt, as if he had been punching a wall. Stay calm, he thought.

Nina remembered the song that began: Count the clouds, the time will come. Then it said something about an eagle. And it ended with all the numbers, one after another, from one to ten. But you could also count to a hundred, or a thousand. She had once counted to two hundred and forty-three. She thought that now she would get up and go and see who those men were and what they wanted. If she couldn't open the trapdoor, she would cry out, and her father would come to get her. But instead she stayed there, lying on her side, her knees pulled up to her chest, her shoes balanced one on top of the other, her cheek feeling the cool of the earth through the rough wool of the blanket. She began to sing the song under her breath, in a thin voice. Count the clouds, the time will come.

'WE meet again, doctor,' Salinas said.

Manuel Roca looked at him without speaking. He pressed a rag against the wound. They had made him sit in the middle of the room, on a wooden chest. El Gurre was behind him, somewhere, gripping his machine gun. They had stationed the boy, Tito, at the door, to see that no one arrived, outside, and every so often he turned, and looked at what was happening in the room. Salinas walked back and forth. A lit cigarette between his fingers. French.

'I've wasted a lot of time on your account, you know?' he said.

Manuel Roca looked up at him.

'Three hundred kilometres to come down here and get you. It's a long way.'

'Tell me what you want and go.'

'What I want?'

'What do you want, Salinas?'

Salinas smiled.

'What did you say?'

'The war is over.'

Salinas stood over Manuel Roca.

'The winner decides when a war is over.'

Manuel Roca shook his head.

'You read too many novels, Salinas. The war is over, that's it, get it?'

'Not yours. Not mine, doctor.'

Then Manuel Roca began to shout that they had better not touch him, they would all end up in jail, they would be caught and would spend the rest of their lives rotting in prison. He shouted at the boy did he like the idea of growing old behind bars counting the hours and giving blowjobs to some repellent killer? The boy looked at him without responding. Manuel Roca shouted that he was an imbecile, they were duping him, screwing up his life. But the boy said nothing.

Salinas smiled. He looked at El Gurre and smiled. He seemed to be enjoying himself. Finally he became serious. He placed himself in front of Manuel Roca and told him to be quiet, once and for all. He put a hand inside his jacket and took out a pistol. Then he told Roca that he needn't worry about them, no one would ever know anything.

'You will disappear into a void, and no one will say a word. Your friends have abandoned you, Roca. And mine are very busy. To kill you will be a favour to everyone. You're screwed, doctor.'

'You're mad.'

'What are you saying?'

'You're mad.'

'Say it again, doctor. I like hearing you talk about madmen.'

'Go fuck yourself, Salinas.'

Salinas released the safety on the pistol.

'Now listen to me, doctor. Do you know how many times I fired a shot in four years of war? Twice. I don't like to shoot, I don't like weapons, I've never wanted to carry one, I don't enjoy killing, I fought my war sitting at a desk. Salinas the Rat, you remember? That's what your friends called me. I screwed them one by one. I deciphered their coded messages and put my spies on them. They despised me and I screwed them. It went like that for four years, but the truth is that I fired only twice. Once was at night, I shot into the darkness at no one, the other was the last day of the war, I shot my brother.

'Listen carefully. We went into that hospital before the army arrived, we wanted to go in and kill all of you, but we didn't find you. You had fled, right? You saw how the wind was blowing, so you took off your jailers' shirts and ran, leaving everything behind, just as it was, beds all over the place, sick people everywhere, even in the corridors. But what I remember most was that we couldn't hear a complaint, not a sound, nothing. I will never forget it, there was an absolute silence. Every night of my life I will hear it, an absolute silence. Those were our friends in the beds, and we were going to free them, we were saving them, but when we arrived they welcomed us in silence, because they didn't even have the strength to cry, and, to tell the truth, they no longer had a desire to live. They didn't want to be saved, this is the truth, you had reduced them to a state where they wanted only to die, as soon as possible, they didn't want to be saved, they wanted to be killed.

'I found my brother in a bed among the others, down in the chapel. He looked at me as if I were a distant mirage. I tried to speak to him but he didn't answer, I couldn't tell if he recognised me. I bent over him. I begged him to answer me, I asked him to tell me something. His eyes were wide open, his breath was very slow, it was like a long death agony. I was leaning over him when I heard his voice say "Please", very slowly, with a superhuman effort—a voice that seemed to come from hell. It had nothing to do with his voice, my brother had a ringing voice, when he spoke it was like laughter, but this was something entirely different. He said "Please" slowly and then after a while he said "Kill me". His eyes had no expression, none, they were like the eyes of someone else, his body was motionless, there was only that very slow breath going up and down.

'I said that I would take him away from there, that it was all over and I would take care of everything, but he seemed sunk back into his inferno—he had returned to where he came from, he had said what he wanted to say and then had gone back to his nightmare. What could I do? I tried to think how I could take him away, I looked around for help, I wanted to take him away from there, I was sure of it, and yet I couldn't move, I couldn't manage to move, I don't know how much time passed, what I remember is that at some point I turned and a few feet away I saw El Blanco, he was standing beside a bed, with the machine gun on his shoulder, and what he was doing was crushing a pillow over the face of a boy, the one lying on the bed.

'El Blanco was crying and crushing the pillow. In the silence of the chapel only his sobs could be heard. The boy wasn't moving, he didn't make a sound, he was going silently, but El Blanco was sobbing, like a child. Then he took away the pillow and with his fingers closed the boy's eyes, and then he looked at me. I was looking at him and he looked at me. I wanted to say What are you doing?, but nothing came out of me, and at that moment someone appeared and said that the army was coming, that we had to get out of there. I felt lost, I didn't want to be found there, I heard the others running along the corridors. I took the pillow from under my brother's head, gently, I looked for a while at those frightened eyes, I placed the pillow on his face, and I began to press, bending over my brother. I pressed my hands down on the pillow, and I felt the bones of my brother's face, there under my hands. One cannot ask a man to do such a thing, they couldn't ask it of me. I tried to resist but at a certain point I stopped. I pulled the pillow away. My brother was still breathing, but it was like something digging up air from the depths of hell. It was terrible— the eyes unmoving, and that rattle. He looked at me and I realised that I was screaming. I heard my voice screaming, but as if from a distance, like a dim and fading lament, I couldn't help it, I was still screaming when I noticed El Blanco. He was beside me, he didn't say anything but he was offering me a gun, while I was crying, and they were all fleeing. We two were inside, he offered me the gun. I took it, and placed the barrel against my brother's forehead and, still screaming, I fired.

'Look at me, Roca. I said look at me. In the whole war I fired twice, the first time it was night, and at no one, the second time I shot at close range, at my brother.

'I want to tell you something. I will shoot one more time, and that will be the last.'

Then Roca began to shout again.

'I had nothing to do with it!'

'You had nothing to do with it?'

'I had nothing to do with the hospital.'

'What the hell are you saying?'

'I did what they told me to do.'

'You...'

'I wasn't there when...'

'What the fuck are you saying?'

'I swear it, I...'

'That was your hospital, you bastard...'

'My hospital?'

'That was your hospital, you were the doctor who was taking care of them, you killed them, you broke them, they were sent to you and you broke them...'

'I never...'

'SHUT UP!'

'I swear to you, Salinas...'

'SHUT UP!'

'I never...'

'SHUT UP!'

Salinas placed the gun against one of Roca's knees. Then he fired. The knee exploded like a piece of fruit. Roca fell back and curled on the ground, shrieking with pain. Salinas was standing over him, he aimed the gun at him and went on shouting.

'I'LL KILL YOU, UNDERSTAND? I'LL KILL YOU, I'M GOING TO KILL YOU.'

El Gurre took a step forward. The boy, at the door, stared in silence. Salinas was shouting, his cream-coloured suit was spattered with blood. He was shouting in a strange, harsh voice, as if he were crying. Or as if he were no longer capable of breathing. He was shouting that he would murder him. Then they all heard an impossible voice say something softly.

'Go away.'

They turned and saw a child, standing on the other side of the room. He was holding a rifle and had it pointed at them. He said again, softly:

'Go away.'

Nina heard the hoarse voice of her father, who was groaning in pain, and then the voice of her brother. She thought that when she came out of there she would go to her brother and would tell him that he had a lovely voice, because it truly seemed lovely to her, so clean and infinitely childlike, the voice she had heard murmur quietly:

'Go away.'

'Who the hell...'

'It's the son, Salinas.'

'What the hell do you mean?'

'It's Roca's son,' El Gurre said.

Salinas cursed, he began shouting:

'THERE WASN'T SUPPOSED TO BE ANYONE HERE, WHAT'S THIS NONSENSE, YOU SAID THERE WASN'T ANYONE.'

He was shouting and didn't know where to point the gun, he looked at El Gurre, and then at Tito, and finally he looked at the child with the rifle and shouted at him that he was a stupid fuck, and that he would never get out of there alive if he didn't put that damn gun down immediately.

The boy remained silent and kept the gun raised.

Then Salinas stopped shouting. His voice came out calm and fierce. He said to the boy that now he knew what sort of man his father was, now he knew that he was an assassin, that he had murdered dozens of people, sometimes he poisoned them little by little, with his medicine, but others he killed by cutting open their chests and then leaving them to die. He said to the child that with his own eyes he had seen boys come from that hospital with their brains blown out. They could hardly walk, they couldn't speak—they were like idiots. He said that his father was called the Hyena, and that it was his friends who called him the Hyena, and they laughed when they said it.

Roca was gasping on the floor. He began to murmur quietly, 'Help,' as if from far away—help, help, help—a litany. He felt death approaching. Salinas didn't even look at him. He went on talking to the child. The child was listening, not moving. Finally Salinas said to him that things were like that, and it was too late to do anything, even with a gun in your hand. He looked him in the eyes, with an infinite weariness, and asked if he understood who that man was, if he truly understood. With one hand he indicated Roca. He wanted to know if the boy understood who he was.

The boy put together everything he knew, and what he understood of life. He answered:

'He's my father.'

Then he fired. A single shot. Into emptiness.

El Gurre responded instinctively. The machine-gun burst lifted the child up off the floor and hurled him at the wall, in a mess of lead, bone and blood. Like a bird shot in mid-flight, Tito thought.

Salinas threw himself to the floor. He ended up beside Roca. For a moment the two men looked at each other. From Roca's throat came a dull, horrible howl. Salinas slid away and rolled onto his back to get Roca's eyes off him. He began to tremble all over. There was a heavy silence. Only that horrible howl. Salinas raised himself up on his elbows and looked at the far end of the room.

The child's body was leaning against the wall, tattered

by the machine-gun volley, ripped open by the wounds. His gun had flown into a corner. Salinas saw that the child's head was upside down, and in his open mouth he saw the little white teeth, a neat white row. Then he let go, falling onto his back. His eyes stared at the ceiling, with its line of beams. Dark wood. Old. He was trembling all over. He couldn't keep his hands still, his legs, nothing.

Tito took two steps towards him.

El Gurre stopped him with a nod.

Roca gave a grim cry, a death cry.

Salinas said softly: 'Make him stop.'

His teeth were chattering, and as he spoke he was trying to stop them.

El Gurre searched his eyes to understand what he wanted.

Salinas's eyes were fixed on the ceiling. A line of dark wood beams. Old.

'Make him stop,' he repeated.

El Gurre took a step forward.

Roca howled, lying in his own blood, his mouth hideously wide.

El Gurre stuck the barrel of the gun in his throat.

Roca kept on howling, against the warm metal of the barrel.

El Gurre fired. A short burst. Dry. The last of his war.

'Make him stop,' Salinas said again.

NINA heard the silence and it frightened her. Then she joined her hands and stuck them between her legs. She curled up even tighter, bringing her knees near her head. She thought now it would all be over. Her father would come to get her and they would go and have supper. She thought they would not speak again of that night, and that soon they would forget about it. She thought this because she was a child and couldn't know.

'The girl,' said El Gurre.

He held Salinas by the arm, to make him stand up. He said to him softly:

'The girl.'

Salinas' gaze was blank.

'What girl?'

'Roca's daughter. If the boy was here she probably is, too.'

Salinas muttered something. Then he shoved El Gurre away. He pulled himself up holding onto the table. His shoes were soaked in Roca's blood.

El Gurre nodded at Tito, then directed him towards the kitchen. When Tito passed the boy on the floor he bent down for an instant and closed his eyes. Not like a father. Like someone who turns off the light as he is leaving a room.

Tito thought of his own father's eyes. One day some men had knocked on the door of his house. Tito had never seen them before. But they said they had a message for him. Then they had handed him a canvas sack. He had opened it and inside were the eyes of his father. 'Take care which side you stand on, kid,' they said. And they went away.

Tito saw a drawn curtain on the other side of the room. He released the safety of his pistol and advanced. He parted the curtain. Behind it was a small room. Everything was in disarray. Chairs overturned, trunks, tools and some baskets of half-rotted fruit. There was a strong smell of food gone bad. And of dampness. On the floor the dust was strange: it looked as if someone had dragged his feet through it. Or something else.

He heared El Gurre on the other side of the house beating the walls with his machine gun, looking for hidden doors. Salinas must still be there, holding onto the table, shaking. Tito moved one of the fruit baskets. He made out the line of a trapdoor. He hit the floor hard with one boot, to hear what noise it made. He moved two more baskets. It was a small trapdoor, carefully cut out. Tito looked up. Through a small window he saw that it was dark outside. He hadn't even realised that it was night. It was time to go, to get away from there. Then he knelt on the floor, and lifted the trapdoor. There was a girl inside, curled up on her side, her hands hidden between her thighs, her head bent forward slightly, towards her knees. Her eyes were open.

Tito pointed his gun at her.

'Salinas!' he shouted.

The child turned her head and looked at him. She had dark eyes, oddly shaped. She looked at him without expression. Her lips were half closed and she was breathing calmly. She was an animal in its den. Tito felt returning to him a sensation he had felt a thousand times, finding that exact position, between the warmth of sheets or under the afternoon sun of childhood. Knees folded, hands between the legs, feet balanced. Head bent forward slightly, closing the circle. How lovely it was, he thought. The child's skin was white, and the outline of her lips perfect. Her legs stuck out from under a short red skirt, as if in a drawing. It was all so orderly. It was all so complete.

Exact.

The girl turned her head back, to its former position. She bent it forward slightly, closing the circle. Tito realised that no one had answered, beyond the curtain. Time had surely passed, and yet no one had answered. He could hear El Gurre banging with his gun against the walls of the house. A muted meticulous sound. Outside it was dark. He lowered the trapdoor. Slowly. He remained there, on his knees, to see if through the cracks he could see the child. He would have liked to think. But he couldn't. Every so often he was too tired to think. He got up. He put the baskets back. He felt his heart banging against his temples.

They went out into the night like drunks. El Gurre

supported Salinas, pushing him forward. Tito walked behind them. Somewhere, the old Mercedes was waiting for them. They went a dozen yards or so without exchanging a word. Then Salinas said something to El Gurre and he went back towards the farmhouse. He didn't seem very certain, but he went back. Salinas leaned on Tito and told him to keep walking. They skirted the woodpile and left the road to take a path that led through the fields. There was a deep silence, and for that reason Tito was unable to say the sentence that he had in mind and had decided to say: 'There is still a child in there.' He was tired, and there was too much silence. Salinas stopped. He was shaking and it was an enormous effort to walk. Tito said something softly, then he turned and looked back. He saw El Gurre running towards them. Behind him he saw the farmhouse rip the darkness, ablaze with the fire that was devouring it. The flames shot up and a cloud of black smoke rose slowly in the night. Tito moved away from Salinas and stood petrified, watching. El Gurre joined them and without stopping said 'Let's go, kid.' But Tito didn't move.

'What the hell did you do?' he said.

El Gurre was trying to drag Salinas away. He said again that they had to go. Then Tito grabbed him by the neck and began to shout in his face, 'What the hell did you do?'

'Calm down, kid,' said El Gurre.

But Tito wouldn't stop, he began shouting louder and louder, 'WHAT THE HELL DID YOU DO?,' shaking El Gurre like a puppet. 'WHAT THE HELL DID YOU DO?,' until Salinas, too, began shouting: 'STOP IT, KID.' They were like three mad men, shouting at each other, abandoned on a dark stage.

Finally they dragged Tito away. The glare of the fire lit up the night. They crossed a field and went down to the road, following the streambed. When they came in sight of the old Mercedes, El Gurre put a hand on Tito's shoulder and said to him softly that he had done a fine job, and that it was all over now. But Tito wouldn't stop repeating the words over and over. He didn't shout. He spoke softly, in a child's voice.

'What the hell have we done? What the hell have we done? What the hell have we done?'

The old farmhouse of Mato Rujo stood blankly in the

countryside, carved in red flame against the dark night. The only stain in the empty outline of the plain.

THREE days later a man arrived, on horseback, at the farmhouse of Mato Rujo. He was filthy, dressed in rags. The horse was an old nag, skin and bones. It had something in its eyes, a yellow liquid that dripped down its muzzle, and the flies buzzed around it.

The walls of the farmhouse stood blackened and useless, coals in the middle of an enormous quenched brazier. They were like the last remaining teeth in the mouth of an old man. The fire had also consumed a large oak that for years had shaded the house. Like a black claw, it stank of calamity.

The man stayed in the saddle. He made a slow half-circle around the farm. He went to the well and, without getting off the horse, unhooked the bucket and let it fall. He heard the slap of metal on water. He looked over at the farmhouse. He saw that sitting on the ground, leaning against what remained of a wall, there was a child. She was staring at him, two motionless eyes shining in a smoke-grimed face. She was wearing a short red skirt. She had scratches all over. Or wounds.

The man pulled up the bucket from the well. The water was blackish. He stirred it with a tin dipper, but the blackness remained. He refilled the dipper, brought it to his lips, and took a long drink. He looked again into the water in the bucket. He spat into it. Then he set everything on the edge of the well and pressed his heels into the belly of the horse.

He went over to the child. She raised her head to look at him. She seemed to have nothing to say. The man studied her for a while. Eyes, lips, hair. Then he held out a hand. She stood, grabbed the man's hand, and pulled herself up, behind him. The old nag adjusted to the new weight. It tossed its head, twice. The man made a strange noise, and the horse calmed down.

As they rode away from the farmhouse, at a slow trot, under a fierce sun, the girl let her head fall forward and, with her forehead against the man's sweaty back, slept.

THE signal changed to green and the woman crossed the street. She looked down as she walked, because it had just stopped raining and in the hollows of the asphalt there were puddles that reminded one of the sudden rain of early spring. She had an elegant gait, confined by the tight black skirt. She saw the puddles and avoided them.

When she reached the opposite pavement she stopped. People passed by, crowding the late afternoon with their steps towards home, or freedom. The woman liked to feel the city trickling around her, so she stood for a while, in the middle of the pavement, inexplicable, like a woman who had been left there, abruptly, by her lover.

She decided to turn right, and fell in with the collective promenade. In no hurry, she went along beside the shop windows, holding a shawl over her chest. She walked tall and confident, with a youthful bearing in spite of her age. Her hair was white, gathered at the nape and held by a dark comb, like a girl's.

She stopped at the window of an appliance shop, and stood staring at a wall of televisions broadcasting pointless multiplications of a single news commentator. Each was tinted a different colour, which fascinated her. A film began of some cities at war and she resumed her walk. She crossed Calle Medina and then the little Plaza del Perpetuo Socorro.

When she arrived at the Galería Florencia she turned to look at the prospect of the lights extending in a line through the belly of the building and out the other side, into Avenida 24 DeJulio. She stopped. She raised her eyes to look for something on the grand iron archway that marked the entrance. But she found nothing. She took a few steps inside the Galería, then stopped a man. She excused herself, and asked him what the place was called. The man told her. She thanked him and said that he would have a most beautiful evening.

The man smiled.

She walked through the Galería Florencia, and eventually she saw, some twenty yards ahead, a small kiosk that stuck out from the left-hand wall, creasing for a moment the clean profile of the space. It was one of those kiosks where lottery tickets are sold. She continued walking, but when she was a few steps from the kiosk she stopped. She saw that the man who sold the tickets was seated, reading a newspaper. He held it resting on something in front of him. All the sides of the kiosk were of glass, except the one against the wall of the Galería. Within, the ticket man could be seen, and a mass of coloured strips hanging down. There was a small window in front, and that was the opening through which the ticket seller talked to people.

The woman pulled back a lock of hair that had fallen over her eyes. She turned and for an instant stood looking at a girl who came out of a shop pushing a baby carriage. Then she looked at the kiosk again.

The ticket seller was reading.

The woman approached and leaned towards the window.

'Good evening,' she said.

The man raised his eyes from the newspaper. He was about to say something, but when he saw the woman's face he stopped, completely. He remained like that, looking at her.

'I would like to buy a ticket.'

The man nodded yes. But then he said something that had nothing at all to do with that.

'Have you been waiting a long time?'

'No, why?'

The man shook his head, continuing to stare at her.

'Nothing, excuse me,' he said.

'I'd like a ticket,' she said.

Then the man turned and stuck his hand up among the strips of tickets hanging behind him.

The woman pointed to a strip that was longer than the others.

'That one there...can you take it from that strip?'

'This one?'

'Yes.'

The man tore off the ticket. He glanced at the number and nodded approval with his head. He placed it on the wooden counter between him and the woman.

'It's a good number.'

'What did you say?'

The man didn't answer because he was looking at the woman's face, as if he were searching for something.

'Did you say it's a good number?'

The man lowered his gaze to the ticket:

'Yes, it has two eights in a symmetrical position and has equal sums.'

'What does that mean?'

'If you draw a line through the middle of the number, the sum of the figures on the right is the same as those on the left. Generally that's a good sign.'

'And how do you know?'

'It's my job.'

The woman smiled.

'You're right.'

She placed her money on the counter.

'You're not blind,' she said.

'I beg your pardon?'

The man began laughing.

'No, I'm not.'

'It's odd...'

'Why should I be blind?'

'Well, the people who sell lottery tickets always are.'

'Really?'

'Maybe not always, but often. I think people like it that they're blind.'

'In what sense?'

'I don't know, I imagine it has to do with the idea of fortune being blind.'

The woman began to laugh. She had a nice laugh, with no sign of age in it.

'Usually they're very old, and they look around like tropical birds in the window of a pet shop.' She said this with great assurance.

Then she added: 'You are different.'

The man said that in fact he was not blind. But he was old.

'How old are you?' the woman asked.

'I'm seventy-two,' said the man.

Then he added: 'This is a good job for me, I have no problems, it's a good job.'

He said it in a low voice. Calmly.

The woman smiled.

'Of course. I didn't mean that...'

'It's a job I like.'

'I'm sure of it.'

She took the ticket and put it in a small black purse. Then she turned around for an instant as if she had to check something, or wanted to see if there were people waiting behind her. At the end, instead of thanking him and leaving, she spoke.

'I wonder if you might like to come and have something to drink with me.'

The man had just put the money into the cash drawer. He stopped with his hand in midair.

'I?'

'Yes.'

'I...I can't.'

The woman looked at him.

'I have to keep the kiosk open, I can't go now, I have no one here that...I...'

'Just a glass.'

'I'm sorry. Really I can't do it.'

The woman nodded yes, as if she had understood. But then she leaned towards the man and said:

'Come with me.'

'Please,' the man said.

'Come with me,' she repeated.

It was strange. The man folded the newspaper and got off the stool. He removed his glasses. He put them in a grey cloth case. Then, very carefully, he began to close the kiosk. He lined up each gesture with the next, slowly, silently, as if it were an ordinary evening.

The woman waited, standing calmly, as if it had nothing to do with her. Every so often someone passed by and turned to look at her. Because she seemed to be alone, and was beautiful. Because she was not young, and seemed alone.

The man turned off the light. He pulled down the little shutter and fastened it to the ground with a padlock. He put on an overcoat, which was loose on his shoulders. He went over to the woman.

'I'm finished.'

The woman smiled at him.

'Do you know where we could go?'

'Over here. There's a café where one can sit quietly.'

THEY went into the café, found a table, in a corner, and sat down across from one another. They ordered two glasses of wine. The woman asked the waiter if he had cigarettes. So they began to smoke. Then they spoke of ordinary things, and of people who win the lottery. The man said that usually they couldn't keep the secret, and the funny thing was that the first person they told was always a child. Probably there was a moral in that, but he had never managed to figure out what it was. The woman said something about stories that have a moral and those that don't. They went on a little like that, talking. Then he said that he knew who she was, and why she had come.

The woman said nothing. She waited.

Then the man went on.

'Many years ago, you saw three men kill your father, in cold blood. I'm the only one of the three who's still alive.'

The woman looked at him. But you couldn't tell what she was thinking.

'You came here to find me.'

He spoke calmly. He wasn't nervous, not at all.

'Now you've found me.'

Then they were silent, because he had no more to say.

'WHEN I was a child my name was Nina. But everything ended that day. No one calls me by that name anymore. I liked it: Nina. Now I have many names. It's different.

'In the beginning I remember a sort of orphanage. Nothing else. Then a man whose name was Ricardo Uribe came and took me away with him. He was the pharmacist in a little town deep in the countryside. He had no wife or relatives, nothing. He told everyone that I was his daughter. He had moved there a few months earlier. Everyone believed him. In the daytime I stayed in the rear of the pharmacy. Between customers he taught me. I don't know why but he didn't like me to go out alone. "What there is to learn you can learn from me," he said. I was eleven. At night he sat on the sofa and made me lie beside him. I rested my head in his lap and listened to him. He told strange stories about the war. His fingers caressed my hair, back and forth, slowly. I felt his sex, under the material of his pants. Then he kissed my forehead and let me go to sleep. I had a room to myself. I helped him keep the shop clean and the house. I washed and cooked. He seemed a good man. He was afraid, but I don't know what he was afraid of.

'One night he leaned over and kissed me on the mouth. He went on kissing me, like that, and meanwhile he stuck his hands under my skirt. I did nothing. And then, suddenly, he pulled away from me, and began to cry and ask me to forgive him. He seemed terrified. I didn't understand. A few days later he said that he had found me a fiancé. A young man from Río Galván, a town nearby. He was a mason. I would marry him as soon as I was old enough. I went to meet him the following Sunday in the square. He was a handsome boy, tall and thin, very thin. He moved slowly, maybe he was sick, or something like that. We introduced ourselves, and I went home.'

THE man thought the way she spoke was strange. As if it were a gesture that she wasn't used to. Or as if she were speaking a language that was not her own. As she searched for words she stared into space.

47

'A few months later, on a winter evening, Uribe went out to the Riviera, a sort of tavern where the men gambled. He went every week, always the same day, Friday.

'That night he played until very late. Then he found himself with four jacks in his hand, in front of a pot in which there was more money than he would see in a year. The game had come down to him and the Count of Torrelavid. The others had put in a little money and then had let it go. But the Count was stubborn. He kept raising the bet. Uribe was sure of his cards and stayed with him. They reached the point where the players lose any sense of reality. And then the Count put in the pot his *fazenda* of Belsito. In the tavern everything came to a halt. Do you gamble?'

'No,' said the man.

'Then I don't think you'll understand.'

'Try me.'

'You won't understand.'

'It doesn't matter.'

'Everything came to a halt. And there was a silence you won't understand.'

The woman explained that the *fazenda* of Belsito was the most beautiful *fazenda* in that land. An avenue of orange trees led to the house at the top of a hill and from there, from the house, you could see the ocean.

'Uribe said that he had nothing to bet that was worth Belsito. And he placed his cards on the table. Then the Count said that he could always bet the pharmacy, and then he began to laugh like a lunatic, and some of those who were there began to laugh with him. Uribe smiled. He still had a hand over his cards. As if to say goodbye to them. The Count became serious again, leaned forward, across the table, looked Uribe in the eye, and said: "You have a lovely child, though."

'Uribe didn't understand right away. He felt all those eyes upon him, and he couldn't think. The Count simplified the situation.

"Belsito against your daughter, Uribe. It's an honest offer."

'And on the table, right under Uribe's nose, he placed his five cards, face down.

'Uribe stared, without touching them. He said something in a whisper, but no one could ever tell me what it was. Then he pushed his cards towards the Count, sliding them across the table.

'The Count came and got me that same night. He did something unpredictable. He waited sixteen months, and when I was fourteen he married me. I gave him three sons.

'Men are difficult to understand. The Count, before that night, had seen me only once. He was sitting in the café and I was crossing the square. He had asked someone: "Who is that girl?" And they told him.'

OUTSIDE it had started raining again, and the café had filled up. One had to speak loudly to be understood. Or sit closer. The man said to the woman that she had an odd way of talking: she seemed to be telling the story of someone else's life.

'What do you mean?'

'It's as if nothing matters to you.'

The woman said that, on the contrary, everything mattered to her, too much. She said that she felt nostalgic for every single thing that had happened to her. But she said it in a hard voice, without melancholy.

Then the man was silent, looking at the people around them. He thought of Salinas. He had been found dead in his bed one morning, two years after that business of Roca. Something with his heart, they said. Then a rumour spread that his doctor had poisoned him, a little every day, slowly, for months. A slow agony. Horrifying. The matter was investigated but nothing came of it. The doctor's name was Astarte. He had made a little money, during the war, with a preparation that cured fevers and infections. He had invented it himself, with the help of a pharmacist. The preparation was called Botrin. The pharmacist was called Ricardo Uribe. At the time he worked in the capital. When the war was over he had had some trouble with the police. First they found his name on the list of suppliers for the hospital of the Hyena, then someone came forward and said he had seen him working there. But many also said that he was a good man.

He presented himself to the investigators and explained everything, and when they let him go he took his things and went away to a small town buried in the countryside, in the south. He bought a pharmacy there, and resumed his profession. He lived alone with a small daughter he called Dulce. He said the mother had died many years earlier. Everyone believed him.

Thus he hid Nina, the surviving daughter of Manuel Roca.

The man looked around without seeing anything. He was in his thoughts.

The savagery of children, he was thinking.

We have turned over the earth so violently that we have reawakened the savagery of children.

He looked back at the woman. She was looking at him.

'Is it true that they called you Tito?' she asked.

The man nodded yes.

'Had you ever met my father before?'

'I knew who he was.'

'Is it true that you were the first to shoot him?'

The man shook his head.

'What difference does it make...'

'You were twenty. You were the youngest. You had been fighting for only a year. El Gurre treated you like a son.'

Then the woman asked if he remembered.

The man stared at her. And only in that instant, finally, did he see again, in her face, the face of that child, lying there, impeccable and right, perfect. He saw those eyes in these, and that extraordinary strength in the calm of this tired beauty. The child: she had turned and looked at him. The child: now she was there. How dizzying time can be. Where am I? the man wondered. Here or there? Have I ever been in a moment that was not this one?

The man said that he remembered. That he had done nothing else, for years, but remember everything.

'For years I asked myself what I ought to do. But the truth is that I never was able to tell anyone. I never told anyone that you were there that night. You may not believe it, but it's so. At first, obviously, I didn't say anything because I was afraid. But time passed, and it became something else. No one thought about the war anymore. People wanted to look ahead, they no longer cared about what had happened. It all seemed to be buried forever. I began to think that it was better to forget everything. Let it go.

'At a certain point, however, it emerged that Roca's daughter was alive, she was hidden somewhere, in a village in the south. I didn't know what to think. It seemed incredible to me that she had come out of that inferno alive, but with children you can never say. Finally someone saw the girl and swore that it was really her. So I realised that I would never be free of that night. Neither I nor the others. Naturally I began to ask myself what she might have seen and heard. And if she could remember my face. Who can know what happens in the mind of a child, confronted by something like that. Adults have a memory, and a sense of justice, and often they have a taste for revenge. But a child? For a while I convinced myself that nothing would happen. But then Salinas died. In that strange way.'

The woman was listening to him, motionless.

He asked if she wanted him to go on.

'Go on,' she said.

'It came out that Uribe had something to do with it.'

The woman looked at him without expression. Her lips were half closed.

'It may have been a coincidence, but certainly it was

odd. Little by little everyone was persuaded that the child knew something. It's difficult to understand now, but those were strange times. The country was going forward, beyond the war, at an incredible speed, forgetting everything. But there was a whole world that had never emerged from the war, and was unable to fit in with that happy land. I was in that world. We all were. For us nothing had ended. And that child was a danger. We talked about it a lot. The fact is that the death of Salinas didn't go down with anyone. So it was decided that somehow the child should be eliminated. I know it seems madness, but in reality it was all very logical: terrible, and logical. They decided to eliminate her and charged the Count of Torrelavid to do it.'

The man paused. He looked at his hands. It was as if he were putting his memories in order.

'He was a man who had been a double agent for the whole war. He worked for them, but he was one of us. He went to Uribe and asked him if he would rather spend his life in jail for the murder of Salinas or vanish into nothing and leave him the child. Uribe was a coward. He had only to stay quiet, and no court would have succeeded in convicting him. But he was afraid and he fled. He left the child to the Count and fled. He died ten years later, in some godforsaken village on the other side of the border. He left a note saying that he had done nothing and that God would follow his enemies to the gates of hell.'

The woman turned to look at a girl who was laughing loudly, leaning on the bar of the café. Then she picked up the shawl that she had hung on the back of the chair and put it over her shoulders.

'Go on,' she said.

'Everyone expected that the Count would have her killed. But he didn't. He kept her with him, at home. They made him understand that he was supposed to kill her. But he did nothing, and kept her hidden in his house. Finally he said: "Don't worry about the girl." And he married her. For months people spoke of nothing else, around there. But then people stopped thinking about it. The girl grew up and bore the Count three sons. No one ever saw her. They called her Doña Sol, because it was the name the Count had given her. One strange thing was said about her. That she didn't speak.

From the time of Uribe, no one had ever heard her say a word. Perhaps it was an illness. Without knowing why, people were afraid of her.'

The woman smiled. She pushed back her hair with a girlish gesture.

IT had grown late and the waiter came and asked if they wanted to eat. In one corner of the café three men had set themselves up and begun to play music. It was dance music. The man said he wasn't hungry.

'I invite you,' the woman said, smiling.

To the man it all seemed absurd. But the woman insisted. She said they could have a dessert.

'Would you like a dessert?'

The man nodded yes.

'All right, then a dessert. We'll have a dessert.'

The waiter said it was a good idea. Then he added that they could stay as long as they wanted. They shouldn't worry about it. He was a young man, and spoke with a strange accent. They saw him turn to the bar and shout the order to someone invisible.

'Do you come here often?' the woman asked.

'No.'

'It's a nice place.'

The man looked around. He said that it was.

'Did your friends tell you all those stories?'

'Yes.'

'And you believe them?'

'Yes.'

The woman said something in a low voice. Then she asked him to tell her the rest.

'What's the point?'

'Do it, please.'

'It's not my story, it's yours. You know it better than I do.'

'Not necessarily.'

The man shook his head. He looked again at his hands.

'One day I took the train and went to Belsito. Many years had passed. I was able to sleep at night and around me were people who didn't call me Tito. I thought I had done it, that the war was really over and there was only one thing left to do. I took the train and went to Belsito, to tell the Count the story of the trapdoor and the child.

He knew who I was. He was very kind, he took me into the library, offered me something to drink, and asked me what I wanted.

'I said, "Do you remember that night, at the farmhouse of Manuel Roca?"

"No," he answered.

"The night when Manuel Roca..."

"I don't know what you're talking about." He said it with great tranquillity, even sweetness. He was sure of himself. He had no doubts.

'I understood. We spoke a little about work and even politics, then I got up and left. He had a young boy take me to the station. I remember because the boy couldn't have been more than fourteen, yet they let him drive the car.'

'Carlos,' said the woman.

'I don't remember his name.'

'My oldest son. Carlos.'

The man was about to say something, but the waiter had come with the desserts. He brought another bottle of wine, too. He said that if they wanted a taste it was a good wine to drink with sweets. Then he said something witty about the owner. The woman smiled, and did it with a movement of her head from which, years earlier, it would have been impossible to defend oneself. But the man barely noticed, because he was following the train of his memories. When the waiter left, he began to speak again.

'Before leaving Belsito that day, as I was walking down the long hallway, with all those closed doors, I thought that somewhere, in the house, you were there. I would have liked to see you. I would have had nothing to say to you, but I would have liked to see your face again, after so many years, and for the last time. I was thinking of that as I was walking down the hallway. And an odd thing happened. At some point one of those doors opened. For a second I was absolutely certain that you would come out, and pass by, without saying a word.'

The man shook his head slightly.

'But nothing happened, because life is never complete—there is always a piece missing.'

The woman, with the spoon in her hand, was staring at the dessert sitting on the plate, as if she were trying to see how to unlock it.

Every so often someone brushed by the table and glanced at the two of them. They were an odd couple. They didn't have the gestures of people who knew each other. But they were speaking intimately. She looked as if she had dressed to please him. Neither of them wore a ring. You would have said they were lovers, but perhaps many years before. Or sister and brother, who could say.

'What else do you know about me?' the woman asked.

The man thought of asking her the same question. But he had begun to tell a story, and he realised that it pleased him to tell it—perhaps he had been waiting years for that moment, to tell it, once and for all, in the shadowy light of a café, with three musicians in a corner, playing the three-four rhythm of dance music learned by heart.

'Some ten years later the Count died in a car accident. You were left with three children, Belsito, and everything else. But the relatives didn't like it. They said you were mad and couldn't be left alone with the three boys. Finally they brought the case to court and the judge concluded that they were right. So they took you away from Belsito and handed you over to the doctors, in a sanatorium in Santander. Is that right?'

'Go on.'

'It seems that your sons testified against you.'

The woman played with her spoon. She made it ring against the edge of the plate.

'A couple of years later you escaped, and disappeared. Someone said it was your friends who had helped you flee, and that now they kept you hidden somewhere. But those who had known you said, simply, that you had no friends. They looked for you for a while. Then they stopped. No one spoke of it anymore. Many were convinced that you were dead. Plenty of crazy people disappear.'

The woman raised her eyes from the plate.

'Do you have children?' she asked.

'No.'

'Why?'

The man answered that one had to have faith in the world to have children.

'In those years I was still working in a factory. Up in the north. They told me that story about you, about the clinic and the fact that you had escaped. They said the most likely thing was that you were at the bottom of a river, or at the foot of a cliff. They told me that it was all over. I thought nothing. It struck me, that business about your being mad, and I remember that I wondered what sort of madness it was: if you wandered around the house screaming, or if you were just silent, in a corner, counting the floorboards and holding a piece of string tight in your hand or the head of a robin. The idea one has of crazy people is ludicrous, if one doesn't know them.'

Then he paused. At the end of the pause he said: 'Four years later El Gurre died.'

Again he fell silent. It was as if it had suddenly become tremendously difficult to go on.

'He was found with a bullet in his back, face down in the manure, in front of his stable.'

He looked up at the woman.

'In his pocket they found a note. On the note was written the name of a woman. Yours.'

He made a light writing motion in the air.

'Doña Sol.'

He let his hand fall back to the table.

63

'It was his handwriting. He had written the name. Doña Sol.'

The three musicians, at the back, struck up a kind of waltz, dragging the tempo and playing very softly.

'From that day I began to expect you.'

The woman had raised her head and was staring at him.

'I knew that nothing could stop you, and that one day you would come to me as well. I never thought that you would shoot me in the back or send someone to kill me who didn't even know me. I knew that you would come and look me in the face, but first you would talk to me. Because I was the one who had opened the trapdoor, that night, and then closed it. And you would not forget that.'

The man hesitated a moment more, then said the only thing he still wanted to say.

'I have carried this secret inside me for my whole life, like a disease. I deserve to be sitting here, with you.'

Then he was silent. He felt his heart beating rapidly, in his fingertips and in his temples. He thought how he was sitting in a café, across from an old woman who was mad and who, from one moment to the next, might get up and kill him. He knew that he would do nothing to stop her.

The war is over, he thought.

THE woman looked around and glanced at her empty plate. She said nothing. From the moment the man had stopped talking she had stopped looking at him. You would have said that she was sitting at the table alone, waiting for someone. The man had let himself fall back into the chair. Now he seemed smaller and tired. He observed, as if from a distance, the woman's eyes wander about the café and over the table: resting everywhere except on him. He realised that he still had his overcoat on, and so he sank his hands in the pockets. He felt the collar pulling at his neck, as if he had put a stone in each pocket.

He thought of the people around, and found it funny how no one, at that moment, could have any idea of what was happening. Seeing two old people at a table one would find it difficult to imagine that at that moment they were capable of anything. And yet it was so. Because she was a phantom and he a man whose life had ended a long time ago. If people knew this, he thought, he would be afraid.

Then he saw that the woman's eyes had become bright. Who could say where the thread of her thoughts was leading.

Her face was without expression. Only, the eyes were at that point.

Was it tears?

He thought again that he wouldn't like to die there, with all those people watching.

Then the woman began to speak.

'Uribe picked up the Count's cards and let them slide slowly between his fingers, revealing them one by one. I don't think he realised at that moment what he was losing. Certainly he realised what he was not winning. I didn't count much for him. He got up and said goodbye to the company, politely. No one laughed, no one dared say a word. They had never seen a poker hand like that. Now, tell me: why should this story be any less true than the one you told?

'My father was a wonderful father. Don't you believe me? And why?—why should this story be less true than yours?

66

'No matter how you try to live just one single life, others will see inside it a thousand more, and this is the reason that you cannot avoid getting hurt.

'Do you know that I know everything about that night, and yet I remember almost nothing? I was there beneath the trapdoor, I couldn't see, I heard something, and what I heard was so absurd, it was like a dream. It all vanished in that fire. Children have a special talent for forgetting. But then they told me, and so I knew everything. Did they lie to me? I don't know. I was never able to ask myself. You came into the house, you fired at him, then Salinas shot him, and finally El Gurre stuck the barrel of the machine gun in his mouth and blew off his head with a short, dry volley. How do I know? He told me. He liked to talk about it. He was an animal. You were all animals. You men always are, in war. How will God forgive you?'

'Stop it.'

'Look at yourself, you seem to be a normal man, you have your worn overcoat, and when you take off your glasses you put them carefully in their grey case. The windows of your kiosk are clean, when you cross the street you look carefully to the right and the left, you are a normal man. And yet you saw my brother die for no reason, only a child with a gun in his hand, a burst of gunfire and he was gone, and you were there, and you did nothing. You were twenty, holy God, you weren't a ruined old man, you were a boy of twenty and yet you did nothing. Please, explain how it is possible. Do you have some way of explaining to me that something like that can happen? It's not the nightmare of a man with a fever, it's something that happened. Can you tell me how it's possible?'

'We were soldiers.'

'What do you mean?'

'We were fighting a war.'

'What war? The war was *over*.'

'Not for us.'

'Not for you?'

'You don't know anything.'

'Then tell me what I don't know.'

'We believed in a better world.'

'What do you mean?'

'You can't turn back. When people begin to murder

each other you can't go back. We didn't want to get to that point, others started it, but then there was nothing else to do.'

'What do you mean a better world?'

'A just world, where the weak don't have to suffer for the evil of the others, where everyone has a right to happiness.'

'And you believed that?'

'Of course I believed it, we all believed it, it could be done and we knew how.'

'You knew?'

'Does that seem so strange to you?'

'Yes.'

'And yet we knew. And we fought for that, to be able to do what was right.'

'Killing children?'

'Yes, if it was necessary.'

'But what are you saying?'

'You can't understand.'

'I can understand—you explain and I'll understand.'

'You can't sow without ploughing first. First you have to break up the earth. First there has to be a time of suffering, do you understand?'

'No.'

'There were a lot of things that we had to destroy in order to build what we wanted, there was no other way, we had to be able to suffer and to inflict suffering— whoever could endure more pain would win, you cannot dream of a better world and think that it will be delivered just because you ask for it. The others would never have given in, we had to fight, and once you understood that it no longer made any difference if they were old people or children, your friends or your enemies, you were breaking up the earth. Then there was nothing but to do it, and there was no way to do it that didn't hurt. And when everything seemed too horrific, we had our dream to protect us. We knew that however great the price the reward would be immense. We were not fighting for money, or a field to work, or a flag. We were doing it for a better world, do you understand what that means? We were restoring to millions of men a decent life, and the possibility of happiness, of living and dying with dignity, without being trampled or scorned. We were nothing, they were everything, millions of men—

we were there for them. What's a boy who dies against a wall, or ten boys, or a hundred? We had to break up the earth and we did, millions of other children were waiting for us to do it, and we did.'

'Do you really believe that?'

'Of course I believe it.'

'After all these years you still believe it?'

'Why shouldn't I?'

'You won the war. Does this seem to you a better world?'

'I have never asked myself.'

'It's not true. You have asked yourself a thousand times, but you're afraid to answer. Just as you have asked yourself a thousand times what you were doing that night at Mato Rujo, fighting when the war was over, killing a man in cold blood whom you had never even seen before, without giving him the right to a trial. Simply killing him, for the sole reason that by now you had begun to murder and were no longer capable of stopping. And in all these years you have asked yourself a thousand times why you got involved in the war, and the whole time your better world is spinning around in your head, so that you will not have to think of the day when they brought you the eyes of your father, or see again all the other murdered men who then, as now, filled your mind, an intolerable memory. That is the only, the true reason you fought, because this was what you had in mind—to be revenged. And now you should be able to utter the word, "revenge". You killed for revenge, you all killed for revenge. It's nothing to be ashamed of, it's the only drug for pain there is, the only way not to go mad, the drug that enables us to fight. But it didn't free you, it burned your entire life, it filled you with ghosts. In order to survive four years of war you burned your entire life...'

'It's not true.'

'You no longer even remember what life is.'

'What do you know about it?'

'Yes, what can I know about it, I'm only a mad old woman, right?, I can't understand, I was a child then, what do I know about it?, I'll tell you what I know, I was lying in a hole, underground, three men came, they took my father, then...'

'Stop it.'

'Don't you like this story?'

'I'm not sorry for anything—we had to fight and we did, we weren't sitting at home with the windows shut, waiting for it to pass, we climbed out of our holes and did what we had to do, that's the truth, you can say anything now, you can find all the reasons you want, but it's different. You had to be there to understand. You weren't there, you were a child. It's not your fault, but you can't understand.'

'You explain, I'll understand.'

'I'm tired now.'

'We have as much time as we want. You talk, I'll listen.'

'Please, leave me alone.'

'Why?'

'Do what you have to do, but leave me in peace.'

'What are you afraid of?'

'I'm not afraid.'

'Then what is it?'

'I'm tired.'

'Of what?'

'Please...'

73

The woman lowered her eyes. She drew away from the table and leaned against the back of the chair. She glanced around, as if suddenly, at that moment, she had realised where she was. The man was kneading his fingers, one hand clasped in the other, but it was the only thing in him that was moving.

At the back of the café, the three musicians played songs from other times. Someone was dancing.

For a while they stayed like that, in silence.

Then the woman said something about a celebration many years earlier, where there was a famous singer who had asked her to dance. In a low voice she told how, though he was old, he moved with astonishing lightness, and before the music ended he had explained to her how a woman's destiny is written in the way she dances. Then he had told her that she danced as if dancing were a sin.

The woman smiled and looked around again.

Then she said something else. It was that evening, at Mato Rujo. She said that when she had seen the trap-door raised she had not been afraid. She had turned to look at the boy's face, and everything had seemed to her very natural, even obvious. She said that in some way she had *liked* what was happening. Then he had lowered the door, and then, yes, she had been afraid, with the worst fear of her life. The darkness that returned, the sound of the baskets dragged over her head again, the boy's footsteps growing distant. She had felt lost. And that terror had never left her. She was silent for a moment and then she added that the mind of a child is strange.

'I think that at that moment,' she said, 'I wished for only one thing: that that boy would take me away with him.'

She went on talking, about children and about fear, but the man didn't hear her because he was trying to put together the words to say one thing he would have liked to let the woman know. He would have liked to tell her that while he was looking at her, that night, curled up in the hole, so orderly and clean—*clean*—he had felt a kind of peace he had never found again, or at least hardly ever, and then it was looking at a landscape, or staring into the eyes of an animal. He would have liked to explain to her exactly that sensation, but he knew the word 'peace' was not enough to describe what he had felt, and yet nothing else occurred to him, except perhaps the idea that it had been like seeing something that was infinitely *complete*. Just as many other times, in the past, he had felt how difficult it was to give a name to what had happened to him in the war, as if there were a spell under which those who had lived couldn't tell the story, and those who knew how to tell the story had not been fated to live.

He looked at the woman and saw her speak, but he didn't hear her because his thoughts again carried him away and he was too tired to resist. So he remained there, leaning back in the chair, and did nothing, until he began to weep. He wasn't ashamed, he didn't hide his face behind his hands, he didn't even try to control his face, contorted in sadness, while the tears descended to his collar, sliding down his neck, which was white and badly shaved, like the neck of every old man in the world.

The woman interrupted. She hadn't realised at first that he had begun to cry, and now she didn't know what to do. She leaned over the table and murmured something, softly. Then instinctively she turned to the other tables and saw that two boys, sitting nearby, were looking at the man, and one of the two was smiling. Then she yelled something at him, and when the boy turned to her, she looked him in the eyes and said to him, loudly:

'Fuck you.'

Then she filled the man's glass with wine and pushed it towards him. She didn't say anything more. She leaned back again. The man continued to weep. Every so often she looked around angrily, like a female animal standing guard at the den of her young.

'WHO are those two?' asked the woman behind the bar.

The waiter knew she was speaking of the two old people, over at the table.

'It's fine,' he said.

'Do you know them?'

'No.'

'The old man was crying, before.'

'I know.'

'They aren't drunk...'

'No, everything's all right.'

'But tell me, why should they come here and...'

To the waiter there didn't seem anything wrong with weeping in a café. But he said nothing. He was the boy with the strange accent. He placed three empty glasses on the bar and went back to the tables.

The woman turned to the old people and watched them for a while.

'She must have been a beautiful woman...'

She said it aloud, even though there was no one to hear her.

When she was young she had dreamed of becoming a movie actress. Everyone said she had wonderful self-confidence, and she liked to sing and dance. She had a pretty voice, rather common but pretty. Then she had met a salesman of beauty products who brought her to the capital to do advertising photos for a night cream. She had sent the photographs home, in an envelope, with some money. For a few months she had tried to succeed with singing, but it didn't work out. Things went better with the ads. Nail polish, lipstick, once some kind of eye drops for redness. She had given up on movies. They said you had to go to bed with everyone, and she didn't want to do that. One day she heard they were looking for TV announcers. She went to a tryout. Since she was wonderfully self-confident and had a pretty, common voice, she passed the first three tryouts and ended up in second place. They told her she could wait, and maybe something would open up. She waited. After two months she got a job doing radio shows, on the first national channel.

One day she went home.

She had married well.

Now she had a café, in the centre of town.

THE woman—the one at the table—leaned forward slightly. The man had stopped crying a little before. He had pulled out of his pocket a big handkerchief and had dried the tears.

'I'm sorry,' he had said.

Then they had said nothing else.

It seemed, indeed, that they no longer had anything to understand together.

And yet at a certain point the woman leaned towards the man again and said: 'I must ask you something a little stupid.'

The man looked up at her.

The woman seemed very serious.

'Would you like to make love to me?'

The man stared at her, motionless, silent.

So the woman was afraid for a moment that she had said nothing, that she had only thought of saying those words without having in fact done so. So she repeated them, slowly.

'Would you like to make love to me?'

The man smiled.

'I'm old,' he said.

'So am I.'

'I'm sorry, but we're old,' the man said again.

The woman realised she hadn't thought about that. Then something else occurred to her and she said:

'I'm not mad.'

'It doesn't matter if you are. Really. To me it doesn't matter. It's not that.'

The woman thought for a moment and then said:

'Don't worry, we can go to a hotel. You can choose it. A hotel that no one knows.'

Then the man seemed to understand something.

'You want us to go to a hotel?' he asked.

'Yes. I would like that. Take me to a hotel.'

He said slowly: 'A hotel room.'

He spoke as if by pronouncing the words it had become easier for him to imagine the room, to see it, to understand if he would like to die there.

The woman said he mustn't be afraid.

'I'm not afraid,' he said.

I will never be afraid again, he thought.

The woman smiled because he was quiet and this seemed to her a way of saying yes.

She looked for something in her bag, then she took out a small purse and pushed it across the table to the man.

'Pay with this. I don't like women who pay in a café, but I invited you. Take this then give it back to me when we're outside.'

The man took the little purse.

He thought of an old man paying with a purse of black satin.

THEY crossed the city in a taxi that seemed new and still had plastic on the seats. The woman looked out the window the whole time. They were streets she had never seen.

They got out in front of a hotel called California. The sign lit up in big red letters, one by one, up the four floors of the building. When the word was complete it shone for a little while, then went out completely and began again from the first letter. C. Ca. Cal. Cali. Calif. Califo. Califor. Californ. Californi. California. California. California. California. Darkness.

They stood there for a little while, one beside the other, looking at the hotel from the outside. Then the woman said, 'Let's go', and moved towards the door. The man followed her.

The desk clerk looked at their papers and asked if they wanted a double room. But without any inflection in his voice.

'Whatever there is,' the woman answered.

They took a room that looked onto the street, on the third floor. The desk clerk apologised that there was no elevator and offered to carry up the suitcases.

'No suitcases. We lost them,' said the woman.

The clerk smiled. He was a good man. He watched them disappear up the stairs and didn't think badly of them.

They went into the room and neither of them made a move to turn on the light. The woman placed her purse on a chair and went to the window. She pushed aside the transparent curtains and looked down for a while, into the street. Occasional cars passed, unhurried. In the wall of the house opposite, lighted windows told the domestic tales of ordinary little worlds—happy or sad. She turned, took off her shawl, and put it on a table. The man was standing in the middle of the room. He was wondering if he should sit on the bed, or maybe say something about the place, that it wasn't bad for example. The woman saw him there, with his overcoat on, and he seemed to her alone and timeless, like a movie hero. She went over, unbuttoned his coat and, slipping it off his shoulders, let it fall to the floor. They were so close. They looked into each other's eyes, truly, for the second time in their lives. Then he slowly leaned over her; he had decided to kiss her on the lips. She didn't move and in a low voice said, 'Don't be silly.'

The man stopped, and he stood like that, leaning slightly forward, in his heart the precise sensation that everything was ending. But the woman slowly raised her arms, and taking a step forward embraced him, first gently, then hugging him to her with irresistible force, until her head rested on his shoulder and her whole body pressed against his. The man's eyes were open. He saw before him the lighted window. He felt the body of the woman who was holding him, and her hands, light, in his hair. He closed his eyes. He took the woman in his arms. And with all his old man's strength he hugged her to him.

When she began to undress she said smiling: 'Don't expect much.'

When he was lying on her, he said smiling: 'You are very beautiful.'

FROM a room nearby came the sound of a radio, just perceptible. Lying on his back, in the big bed, completely naked, the man stared at the ceiling wondering if it was weariness that made his head spin, or the wine. Beside him the woman was still, her eyes closed, turned towards him, her head on the pillow. They held each other by the hand. The man would have liked to hear her speak again, but he knew there was nothing more to say, and that any words would be ridiculous at that moment. So he was silent, letting sleep confuse his ideas, and bring back to him the dim memory of what had happened that evening. The night outside was illegible, and the time in which it was vanishing was without measure. He thought that he should be grateful to the woman, because she had led him there by the hand, step by step, like a mother with a child. She had done it wisely, and without haste. Now what remained to be done would not be difficult.

He held her hand, in his, and she returned his clasp. He would have liked to turn and look at her but then what he did was let go of her hand and roll onto his side, giving her his back. It seemed to him that it was what she was expecting from him. Something like a gesture that left her free to think, and in a certain way give her some solitude in which to decide the final move.

He felt that sleep was about to carry him off. It occurred to him that he didn't like being naked because they would find him like that and everyone would look at him. But he didn't dare tell the woman. So he turned his head towards her, not enough to see her and said:

'I'd like you to know that my name is Pedro Cantos.'

The woman repeated it slowly.

'Pedro Cantos.'

The man said:

'Yes.'

Then he laid his head on the pillow again and closed his eyes.

Nina continued to repeat the name in her mind. Without corners, it slid away, like a glass marble. On an inclined tray.

She turned to look at her purse, sitting on a chair, near the door. She thought of going to get it, but she didn't, and remained lying on the bed. She thought of the ticket kiosk, of the waiter in the café, of the taxi with the plastic-covered seats. She saw again Pedro Cantos weeping, his hands sunk in the pockets of his overcoat. She saw him as he caressed her without the courage to breathe. I will never forget this day, she said to herself.

Then she turned, moved closer to Pedro Cantos, and did what she had lived for.

She curled up behind him: she pulled her knees up to her chest; aligned her feet until she felt her legs perfectly paired, the two thighs softly joined, the knees like two cups balanced one on the other, the calves separated by nothing; she shrugged her shoulders slightly and slid her hands, joined, between her legs. She looked at herself. She saw an old doll.

She smiled. Shell and animal.

Then she thought that however incomprehensible life is, probably we move through it with the single desire to return to the hell that created us, to live beside whoever, once, saved us from the inferno. She tried to ask herself where that absurd faithfulness to horror came from but found that she had no answers. She understood only that nothing is stronger than the instinct to return, to where they broke us, and to replicate that moment forever. Only thinking that the one who saved us once can do it forever. In a long hell identical to the one from which we came. But suddenly merciful. And without blood.

The sign outside told its rosary of red lights. They were like the flames of a house on fire.

Nina rested her forehead against Pedro Cantos's back. She closed her eyes and slept.